Daisy
the Festival
Fairy

To Isla, with much love

Special thanks to
Rachel Elliot

ORCHARD BOOKS
338 Euston Road, London NW1 3BH
Orchard Books Australia
Level 17/207 Kent Street, Sydney, NSW 2000
A Paperback Original

First published in 2015 by Orchard Books

HiT entertainment

A CIP catalogue record for this book is available
from the British Library.

ISBN 978 1 40833 651 9

1 3 5 7 9 10 8 6 4 2

Printed and bound by CPI Group (UK) Ltd, Croydon, CR0 4YY

MIX
Paper from
responsible sources
FSC® C104740
www.fsc.org

The paper and board used in this book are made from wood from responsible sources.

Orchard Books is an imprint of Hachette Children's Group
and published by The Watts Publishing Group Limited, an Hachette UK company.

www.hachette.co.uk

Daisy
the Festival
Fairy

by Daisy Meadows

ORCHARD

www.rainbowmagic.co.uk

The
Helter-skelter

Jack Frost's
Ice Castle

Silver Birch
Family Campsite

RAINBOW DAYS
FESTIVAL FIELD

Jack Frost's Spell

The humans love their festivals.
The fairies love them too.
I'll put a stop to all their fun,
And make my dreams come true.

My magic storm will freeze them all,
And send the sun away.
Bring mud and rain and misery,
And fill them with dismay!

The Good-Times Glowstick

Contents

Tents and Tepees

"Get ready for a bumpy ride!" said Mr
Walker.

Rachel Walker and her best friend
Kirsty Tate giggled as the car drove
through an uneven field. They were both
fizzing with excitement.

"I can't believe we really have tickets for the Rainbow Days Festival!" said Rachel. "I keep thinking I must be dreaming."

The festival was so popular that tickets sold out very quickly. The Walkers had always wanted to go, but this was the first time they had been successful.

"What are you looking forward to most, girls?" asked Mrs Walker, turning to smile at them.

"Dressing up!" said Rachel at once. "I love the way that each day has a colourful theme – today is a circus theme, Saturday is carnival and Sunday is 80s fashion."

"I can't wait for the music concerts each day," said Kirsty. "Lots of our favourite groups are going to be here,

like The Angels and Groove Gang and
Jacob Bright."

"But hopefully *not* the Gobolicious
Band," said Rachel in a quiet voice.

Kirsty grinned and crossed her fingers.

They were the only humans who knew
that Frosty and his Gobolicious Band
were Jack Frost and his goblins in
disguise. Jack Frost was always trying to
make trouble for the fairies, and Rachel
and Kirsty had often helped their fairy
friends to foil his plans.

"Look!" said Kirsty, as the car bounced over a particularly large bump. "There's the family camping area."

She pointed to a grassy space full of tents, which was surrounded by a circle of silver birch trees. Someone had painted a large sign on a piece of driftwood:

**Welcome to the
Silver Birch Family Campsite**

Mr Walker parked the car next to a small tepee with the number 11 painted on the side. Then he turned to look at the girls.

"Surprise!" he said. "We're going to sleep in our ordinary tent, but we've hired a tepee for you girls as a special treat."

Rachel undid her seatbelt and flung
her arms around her dad.

"That's amazing, thank you!" she
exclaimed.

"Thank you, Mr and Mrs Walker!"
Kirsty added. "This weekend just gets
better and better!"

The best friends jumped out of the car and pulled their bags out of the boot.

"Let's go and unpack," said Rachel. "I can't wait to see what it's like!"

They ducked their heads to go inside, and both said, "Ooh!" at the same time. The tepee was filled with velvety throws,

cushions and sheepskins. Two thick mattresses lay on the floor, and a rainbow mobile hung from the top. The floor was covered with a thick woven rug.

"I love it!" said Rachel, running inside and twirling around with her arms outstretched. "I wish I could sleep in one all the time!"

There was a list of events pinned to the wall of the tepee. Rachel and Kirsty quickly unpacked their things and then sat down to look at the list.

FRIDAY – Circus Day

Roll up to the circus and prepare to be amazed!

SATURDAY – Carnival Day

It's party time – eat, drink and have fun!

SUNDAY – 80s Fashion Day

Enjoy our biggest music concert ever!

Rainbow Days Festival Fun

Theatre

Dressing-up

Fairground rides

Storytelling

Play areas

Music/craft workshops

Food stalls

Music concerts

And fantastic food stalls!

"Shall we go and look around right now?" said Kirsty.

Rachel popped her head out of the tepee and saw her parents setting up their tent.

"Is it OK if we go and explore?" she called.

"Of course," said Mrs Walker. "We'll meet you back here at lunchtime, OK?"

Rachel agreed, and she and Kirsty quickly pulled on their colourful circus outfits. Rachel had a glittery purple waistcoat with a stripy skirt, and Kirsty chose a dress covered with multi-coloured spots. Then they raced towards the main festival area.

A Magical Ride

The festival field was packed with
children dressed up in bright clothes, and
exciting workshops, rides and activities.
The girls stopped opposite the stripy big
top and looked around. The air was
filled with the aromas of hot doughnuts,

sweet candyfloss and hotdogs, and they could hear the sizzle of frying onions, the dramatic voices of storytellers and the happy squeals of children on fairground rides. A fire juggler was throwing flaming torches high into the air beside the big top.

"I can't decide where I want to go first!" said Rachel with a laugh.

"I can," said Kirsty, grinning.

She pointed to an enormous orange-and-white helter-skelter, which rose high above the other rides and activities. A

22

huge smile spread over Rachel's face and together the best friends raced towards the ride. A few seconds later they were standing at the top.

"Let's go down together," said Kirsty, picking up a mat.

Kirsty sat in front with Rachel's arms around her shoulders and they pushed off down the slide. They whizzed faster…and faster… until everything around them was such a blur that it seemed to sparkle. Rachel

23

squealed and shut her eyes.

"I've never been on such a long helter-skelter!" cried Kirsty. "Wheeeee!"

They shot off the bottom of the slide and landed on a bed of springy heather. To their amazement, they saw that they were no longer at the festival. They weren't even in the human world.

"Welcome to Fairyland," said a tinkling voice.

The girls had landed in the garden beside the Fairyland Palace. A figure was standing in front of them, her crown sparkling in the sunlight.

"Queen Titania!" said Rachel in astonishment.

The girls scrambled to their feet and curtsied to the queen, who smiled at them.

"Welcome, Rachel and Kirsty," she said. "I'm sorry to bring you here so suddenly! But when I realised that you were at the Rainbow Days Festival, I felt sure that you would be able to help Daisy the Festival Fairy."

A fairy peeped out at them from behind the queen's back, and then gave them a friendly smile.

"Hello, I'm Daisy," she said, stepping into view.

A daisy chain was looped through her silky hair, and her colourful clothes would have fitted in well at the Rainbow Days Festival.

"Hello," said Kirsty, smiling back at her. "Why did the queen say that you need our help?"

"I've been organising the first-ever Grand Fairy Festival," said Daisy. "But Jack Frost got bored of all the talk of festivals. Besides, he doesn't like the idea of fairies having fun!"

"What has he done?" asked Rachel with a frown.

"He's stolen my magical objects," Daisy replied. "Without them I can't stop his spells or put on the Fairy Festival."

"What are your magical objects?" asked Kirsty.

"There's the blue good-times glowstick, which makes sure that people have fun, even if the weather isn't nice," said Daisy. "The purple sweet-dreams sleeping bag keeps all tents warm, dry and cosy, and the red VIP wristband helps the booked acts turn up on time and be at their best for their performances."

"I'm hoping that you will be able to help Daisy," said Queen Titania.

"Of course we will," Rachel replied at once. "We'll help however we can."

The queen smiled at them, and Daisy fluttered into the air, clapping her hands together.

"Now I must return you to the human world," said Queen Titania to the girls. "Daisy will find you there."

"See you soon!" called Daisy.

The queen waved her wand, and Rachel and Kirsty were lifted into the air by a flurry of fairy dust. It whizzed them around so fast that they were dazzled by sparkles.

Seconds later the sparkles cleared, and
they were zooming off the end of the
helter-skelter.

"I feel dizzy!" said Rachel, standing up
and then staggering sideways.

"Me too," said Kirsty, as her legs
wobbled underneath her. "I wonder
where Daisy will meet us!"

Clowning Around

The girls knew that Daisy would find them when she was ready, so they decided to pass the time by going to the circus show. The circus master was standing outside the big top, wearing a top hat and a cape with a red lining.

"Roll up, roll up!" he shouted to the crowds. "The best and most exciting circus show in the world is about to start! Don't miss this once-in-a-lifetime opportunity! Gasp at the fire jugglers! Be amazed by the trapeze artists! The show starts in five minutes!"

"That sounds like fun," said Rachel. "Let's go and watch."

Inside the stripy big top, tiers of seats were quickly filling up with people. Kirsty and Rachel found places on the middle row and looked down at the circus ring. The ground was covered with sawdust, and as they watched there was an explosion of silver confetti, a blast of music and three clowns cartwheeled into the ring. Everyone clapped as they faced the audience and started to do tricks.

Boom! There was an explosion of golden confetti and more clowns tumbled into the ring, alongside three unicyclists. There were so many funny and amazing tricks to watch that the girls hardly knew which way to look.

"I need three heads to be able to see everything!" said Kirsty with a laugh.

Rachel laughed too, and then stopped suddenly and leaned forward to stare at two of the clowns' feet.

"Those knobbly green shoes are funny," she said.

Kirsty drew in her breath sharply.

"They're not shoes," she exclaimed. "They're feet…goblin feet!"

The two clown-goblins scurried away from the ring, and the girls saw them slip out of the big top.

"Let's follow them," said Rachel. "I bet they're up to mischief."

She and Kirsty dashed after the goblins, who hurried around to the back of the big top, out of sight of the festival crowds. Rachel was in the lead, and she

stopped so suddenly that Kirsty bumped
into her.

"What's wrong?" she whispered,
peering over Rachel's shoulder.

The goblins had joined six others, who
were standing in a

circle. There
was a hippy
in the
middle of
the circle,
dressed
in a tie-
dye blue
T-shirt
and purple
flares
with a
satchel over his

shoulder. He turned his head to look at the goblins who had just arrived, and the girls recognised Jack Frost!

"Where have you nincompoops been?" he snapped at the clown-goblins. "And what are you wearing?"

"We're the coolest clowns in the circus!" the goblins squawked.

"Shut up and listen," said Jack Frost.

"I've got a job for you lot."

He opened the satchel and pulled out a blue glowstick, a red wristband and a neatly rolled purple sleeping bag.

"Daisy's magical objects!" Kirsty whispered.

"I'm going to have fun this summer," said Jack Frost with an unpleasant grin. "I'm going to spoil every single festival, starting with Rainbow Days."

"How can this stuff help?" asked one of the goblins, prodding the sleeping bag with a bony finger. "How do they work?"

"I don't know how to use them, and I don't care," snapped Jack Frost. "But as long as that pesky Festival Fairy doesn't have them, she can't stop me messing with the weather."

He passed the magical objects to three of the goblins and rubbed his hands together.

"What's the weather got to do with it?" asked another goblin.

Jack Frost cackled.

"I'm going to make the weather so awful that all the festivals will be washed away," he said. "I want you to hide these things where the fairies will never find them — and make as much mischief as you can along the way!"

A Chill in the Air

Rachel and Kirsty were horrified to hear Jack Frost's plans. The goblins didn't look very pleased about it either.

"Why should *we* have to do all the hard work?" grumbled one of the goblins.

"Because I'm going to be busy plotting my most devious spells to bring the worst

weather to the festival!" bellowed Jack
Frost. "Do as you're told and hide those
magical objects. Without them, there's
nothing the fairies can do to block my
spells!"

"We have to stop
them," Kirsty
whispered.

"We can't do
anything at the
moment," said
Rachel. "There are
eight goblins *and* Jack

Frost – we could never get Daisy's things
back without being caught."

The goblins split into three groups,
and each group took one of the
magical objects and ran off. Jack Frost
disappeared in a flash of blue lightning.

"What shall we do?" cried Kirsty.

"Maybe we should go to Fairyland to fetch Daisy," Rachel said.

But Kirsty shook her head.

"If we do that we might never find the goblins," she said. "Let's follow the clowns – at least we might be able to get the good-times glowstick back."

They raced after the clown-goblins, who lifted the edge of the big top and scurried under. Rachel and Kirsty

hurried back to the entrance and found a queue of people. As they stood there, they started to shiver. A chilly breeze whipped up their hair and made their eyes water. All around them, smiles disappeared from people's faces.

"What awful weather," complained a young woman ahead of them.

"This will ruin everything," said a grey-haired man.

"The festival will be spoiled," said another woman. "I'm not queuing up here – it'll probably be a disappointment anyway."

"Remember what Daisy said?" said Rachel under her breath. "The blue glowstick makes sure that people have fun no matter what the weather is like."

"You're right," said Kirsty with a groan. "Now the goblins have it, Jack Frost is using the weather to make everyone feel miserable."

The queue thinned out as people left, looking unhappy. The girls hurried back inside and found that the audience was still cheering the performances and looking happy.

"That's good," said Rachel. "They won't be affected by the weather until they leave the big top."

Around the arena, lots of different performers were entertaining the audience. Clowns, fire jugglers, acrobats and tightrope walkers were making people gasp and applaud, and the girls quickly spotted the clown-goblins. They were throwing buckets of water at each other and trying to trip up the acrobats.

"How can we get nearer to the goblins?" Rachel wondered aloud. "Look – one of them has tucked the glowstick behind his ear. If only we could get close enough to take it back!"

Just then, they heard a yelp from someone nearby. One of the real clowns had thrown a water bomb into the audience! People giggled and squealed as the clowns threw more water bombs.

"Look out!" cried Kirsty. "There's one coming straight at us!"

The water bomb hit Rachel's head and exploded – but instead of icy water the girls were showered with

rainbow-coloured sparkles. They gasped and laughed, and then gasped again.

Daisy the Festival Fairy was fluttering among the sparkles!

A Fairy in the Big Top

In a flash, the little fairy darted out of sight under Rachel's plaits.

"I'm sorry I've been so long," she said. "There's so much to do to prepare for the Fairy Festival – especially now my magical objects are missing. Have you had any ideas about how to find them?"

"Better than that," said Kirsty. "The good-times glowstick is right here in the big top!"

Quickly, the girls explained what had happened and what they had heard of Jack Frost's plans.

"Oh no," said Daisy with a groan. "Part of the experience of festivals is a bit of mud and rain, and my good-times glowstick helps people to see the fun side of that."

"Let's keep our eyes on the goblins," said Rachel. "Perhaps we'll be lucky and one of them will drop it."

But as she
spoke, the
taller goblin
took the
glowstick
from
behind
his ear
and threw it
at the shorter
goblin. They carried
on throwing it to each other, faster and
higher, and suddenly Kirsty had an idea.

"Daisy, if the goblins threw the
glowstick high enough, could you catch
it in the air?" she asked.

Daisy clapped her hands together.

"Yes, definitely!" she said. "But how
can we make them throw it so high?"

"Leave that to Rachel and me," said
Kirsty with a smile.

Daisy zoomed
upwards to the
highest part of the
big top, and then
Kirsty cupped her
hands around her
mouth.

"You're not very
good throwers," she
called to the clown-goblins.

"How dare you?" squawked the taller
goblin. "We're the best throwers in the
whole circus, *actually.*"

"Prove it!" Rachel called out. "How
high can you throw that glowstick?"

"Higher than *you,*" yelled the shorter
goblin, sticking his tongue out at her.

He tossed the glowstick up so high that
it nearly touched the tightrope…and
Daisy swooped down from the flying
trapeze and caught
it with a grin of
triumph. It
immediately
shrank back
to fairy size.

"No!"
squealed
the goblins,
leaping
into the
air as if
they could
jump up high
enough to catch
her.

"Let's go!" Kirsty exclaimed, pulling Rachel to her feet.

They rushed out of the big top again, and seconds later Daisy came darting after them, clutching the glowstick.

"I can't believe it!" she said, hiding under a lock of Kirsty's hair. "You're both so kind – thank you so much for helping me!"

Rachel and Kirsty couldn't stop smiling. Without the glowstick, Jack Frost would find it a lot harder to ruin

festivals. There was still a cool breeze
that made them shiver, but now, it
wasn't spoiling anyone's fun.

"Look at their faces," said Rachel.
"People are smiling again!"

"They've decided that the weather
won't stop them enjoying themselves,"
said Daisy. "And it's
all thanks to you.
You girls are
wonderful!"

"We're so
happy we
could help,"
said Kirsty.

"I just hope
we can find your
other objects too,"
Rachel added.

"I have to take the glowstick back to Fairyland now," said Daisy. "But I'll be back as soon as I can to help you search."

With a flash of her sparkling smile, Daisy disappeared back to Fairyland. The girls shared a hug and then Rachel looked over at the helter-skelter.

"One thing's for sure," she said. "That was definitely the best helter-skelter ride I've ever had!"

The
Sweet-Dreams
Sleeping Bag

Contents

Cloudy Weather

Rachel and Kirsty woke up early on Saturday morning. The first thing they heard was merry birdsong coming from the silver birch trees around their campsite.

"My first night in a tepee," said Kirsty, stretching and gazing around at the cone-shaped walls. "I love it!"

"I dreamed about Daisy," said Rachel. "I hope we can help her to find her other magical objects before Jack Frost spoils everything."

"We still have to find the sweet-dreams sleeping bag and the VIP wristband," said Kirsty, jumping up and starting to get dressed. "I wonder if the goblins who are hiding them are still here at the festival."

Just then there was a crackle outside, and then the girls heard the tinny sound of Mr Walker's portable radio. He had turned on the weather report.

"And it's good news for all you festival-goers," said the weatherman. "We're in for a super-sunny weekend, so don't forget to pack your sun cream!"

The girls exchanged happy smiles.

"That sounds great," said Rachel. "If it's sunny, perhaps that means Daisy has managed to get her magical objects back. She said that they would help her to stop Jack Frost's bad weather spells."

Feeling hopeful, the girls finished getting dressed in their colourful carnival outfits. Then they pushed their way out of the tepee. They were expecting to feel the warm sun on their faces, but the day was grey and a bit chilly.

"Good morning!" called Mr Walker, waving a spatula at them.

He and Mrs Walker were sitting on a camping stool outside their tent, cooking sausages and listening to the radio.

"Funny weather," said Mr Walker, pointing at the sky with his spatula. "The weatherman's got it completely wrong."

A large, dark cloud was sitting above the festival site. The girls looked up at it and then exchanged a worried glance.

"Jack Frost's spell has made that cloud," whispered Kirsty. "He's trying to turn the weather so bad that it spoils the festival for everyone."

Before Rachel could reply, there was a yell from the family camping next to them as their tent collapsed. Then another family's awning ripped in two.

"These sausages still aren't cooked," said Mrs Walker in a surprised voice. "They've been in the pan for half an hour!"

70

"I'll swap our camping stove for yours," called a man opposite them. "Ours is burning everything in seconds!"

"This must be happening because the sweet-dreams sleeping bag is missing," said Rachel. "It keeps tents warm, dry and cosy, remember? I bet it makes sure that people have fun camping too."

"Jack Frost is so mean!" Kirsty exclaimed. "Why does he always want to make other people miserable?"

"Girls, I think you had better go and get some breakfast from one of the food stalls," said Mrs Walker. "Our camping stove isn't working."

"OK," called the girls. "See you later!"

They left the campsite and walked through the fairground area, past the helter-skelter that had taken them to Fairyland yesterday. The rides weren't open yet, but the delicious smell of freshly cooked food wafted towards them from the food stalls further on.

72

Even though it was early, the stalls were crowded with people. For a while the girls forgot about their breakfast, because they were so interested in all the different costumes. As it was Carnival Day, all the festival-goers were dressed in bright, colourful outfits.

"Everyone must be having trouble cooking their own food this morning," said Rachel.

"I hope the stalls don't run out of food," Kirsty replied.

"It looks as if that one might," said Rachel, pointing to the busiest, most crowded of all the stalls.

Just at that moment, a gap appeared in the crowd and the girls saw the two people who were running the stall. They were easy to spot, because they were wearing just one colour – green. They had on caps and baggy shirts, but their disguise didn't fool the girls for an instant. Rachel and Kirsty clutched at each other in alarm.

"GOBLINS!" they exclaimed.

Breakfast – Goblin-style!

The girls hurried closer to the goblin food stall. They stopped next to a lemonade stand and watched the goblins as they served bacon-and-egg rolls to their customers.

"They haven't washed their hands," said Kirsty, noticing the goblins' grubby fingernails.

"It's not even a proper stall," added Rachel. "They've just set up their camping stove next to their tent."

"Who cares?" replied a man nearby. "They're making the most delicious food at the whole festival!"

"It does smell amazing," Kirsty agreed, as the scent wafted under her nose. "It's making my stomach rumble!"

As the girls watched, even more people joined the crowd around the stall, waving their money in the air. The other stalls were almost empty now, and the stallholders were looking upset. They had piles of food but no customers.

"No one wants their lovely food," said Rachel.

The man selling Cornish pasties called out to the goblins, "Excuse me, you have

78

to get permission and a special licence to sell food here."

"Push off," shouted one of the goblins.

"We don't care," said the other.

The first goblin ran over to the Cornish-pasty stall and threw several of the pasties at the other stallholders. Then he began to juggle with them.

"Stop it!" cried the Cornish-pasty man. "That's not fair!"

"Loser, loser!" jeered the first goblin, jangling his moneybag at the man.

The girls were horrified to see the goblins causing such trouble and upset.

"We have to stop them being so rude and naughty," said Kirsty. "What can we do?"

"I can't think of a single plan," said Rachel with a groan. "This is awful."

Just then, out of the corner of her eye, she saw something glimmering. One of the jugs of lemonade on the nearby stall was glowing brightly. She nudged Kirsty, who gave a hopeful smile.

"Is it magic?" she whispered.

"It certainly is," said Daisy, popping her head around the side of the jug. "Hello, girls!"

"Daisy, thank goodness you're here," Rachel exclaimed.

81

"There are some goblins selling food over there, and they're stealing customers from all the other stalls and being really rude."

"Their food smells incredible," Kirsty added. "I didn't think goblins could cook like that."

"Usually they can't," said Daisy, looking serious. "They must have my sweet-dreams sleeping bag! It keeps tents warm and dry, and makes sure campers are well fed. It's the only way that the goblins could be making such delicious food."

Kirsty looked at the goblins. They were serving their food from a rickety-looking table. Close behind them was a small green tent, covered in food stains.

"Perhaps if we creep around the back we could search the tent while the goblins are serving," she suggested. "I bet the sleeping bag is in there."

"Good thinking!" said the little fairy.

She slipped under Rachel's collar. Then the girls walked around the stall in a wide circle so that the goblins wouldn't spot them.

"Maybe we could find the sleeping bag without the goblins realising," said Rachel.

But when they reached the front of the tent, they saw a goblin sitting cross-legged in the entrance. He glared at them.

"What are you staring at?" he squawked.

The girls bent down as if to tie up their shoes and exchanged worried looks.

"What do we do now?" Kirsty whispered. "If we can't get past the guard, we'll never get the sweet-dreams sleeping bag back!"

Fairy Hunter

"We're not giving up," said Rachel.
"I've got an idea. Daisy, please could
you turn us into fairies? If we're small
like you, we can slip under the top sheet
of the tent from the side and then get
inside behind the guard goblin's back."

"That's a great plan, Rachel," exclaimed Daisy, clapping her hands together. "But you will need to find somewhere to hide while I transform you."

Looking around, the girls realised that she was right. There were people everywhere. Then Kirsty spotted an ancient oak tree nearby.

"That tree has an enormous trunk," she said. "No one will spot us behind there."

Quickly they darted over to the tree and slipped behind its wide trunk. Daisy fluttered out from Rachel's collar, holding up her wand. She waved it over the girls, and a glittering shower of fairy dust sprinkled their heads and shoulders. Kirsty gave a shiver of excitement as she

and Rachel shrank
to fairy size, and
then shook
magical dust
from their
fluttering
wings.

"I love
being a fairy,"
said Rachel,
peeping out from
behind the tree at the bustling crowds.
"Isn't it amazing how big humans look
when you're this small?"

Kirsty was gazing at a scattering of
acorn cups under the tree.

"I love being little enough to sit inside
those," she said. "No wonder fairies
always seem so happy!"

"Let's go," said Daisy. "We have to get into the tent before the goblins stop serving food!"

They zoomed towards the tent. Now that they were so small, it was easy to creep under the top sheet,  flutter behind the goblin and into the tent without being spotted.

"What a mess!" whispered Daisy when they got inside and looked around. "Goblins obviously don't care for their belongings very well."

Sleeping bags, pillows and blankets

were piled up around the tent, covered
with half-eaten food. Drinks had been
spilled over everything, leaving sticky,
multi-coloured stains. The goblins
hadn't bothered to clean their feet before
coming into the tent, so there were large,
muddy footprints everywhere.

"How can we find anything in here?"
asked Rachel in a low voice. "It's a tip!"

"We'll just have to tidy up," Daisy replied. "I'm afraid we'll have to do it the human way, though – we can't risk the guard goblin noticing flashes of fairy magic."

The three friends started with the nearest pile. They lifted pillows and folded blankets by each taking a corner. Then, underneath an empty sweet packet, Kirsty spotted the corner of a purple sleeping bag.

"There it is!" she said in an excited squeak. "We've found it!"

"I don't think so!" squawked a voice from behind them.

They twirled around and saw the guard goblin standing in the entrance. He grabbed an empty pillowcase.

"Time for a bit of fairy hunting!" he yelled.

He zipped up the tent entrance behind him and then lunged at them like a butterfly hunter with a net.

In a panic, the fairies flew left and right, trying to find a way to escape. But the goblin kept blocking their path, and at last he managed to force them to fly into the corner of the tent. Then he pounced, and the fairies darted backwards, bumped into the canvas and bounced off it again – straight into the goblin's waiting pillowcase!

"Got you!" he crowed in delight.

He clutched the pillowcase shut with one hand. Rachel, Kirsty and Daisy kicked and beat their hands against it, but it was no use.

They were trapped!

A Pillowy Prison

"Let us out!" Rachel cried out. "You can't keep us prisoners here!"

"Oh yes I can!" yelled the goblin. "I can do whatever I want because I'm bigger than you!"

"That's ridiculous," Kirsty exclaimed. "You're just being a big bully."

"You can stay in there until all our food is sold," said the goblin. "Then I'm taking you straight to Jack Frost, and he'll lock you up in the Ice Castle!"

He shook the pillowcase and the fairies tumbled around, feeling dizzy.

"Try to hover!" called Daisy.

But with the cloth flopping around them, it was impossible to stay upright or keep flying. They were bumped and somersaulted around until it seemed as if everything was spinning.

98

When the goblin finally put the
pillowcase down, the material drooped
on top of them, as heavy as a blanket.
They couldn't see each other. They
couldn't see *anything*.

"You're not getting away from me,"
squawked the goblin. "I'm the cleverest
goblin in the Ice Castle, and I'm going
to prove it. I'll be the very first goblin to
give Jack Frost three fairy prisoners!"

Lying under the heavy cloth, Rachel,
Kirsty and Daisy felt something thump
down beside them.

"Can you hear me?" whispered Daisy. "Are you OK?"

In the darkness, Rachel and Kirsty breathed sighs of relief.

"I'm OK," said Rachel.

"Me too," said Kirsty. "But how are we going to get out?"

"He's put something over the neck of the pillowcase," said Daisy. "Silly goblin – he's forgotten that I have a wand. As soon as he's gone I can use magic to set us free."

But then Rachel and Kirsty heard her groan.

"My wand!" she cried. "I've dropped it!"

"It must be in here somewhere," said Kirsty.

She lifted the cloth and peered around. Everything was shadowy and it was hard to see anything.

"Do you think he's gone?" Rachel asked. "We have to try to push whatever it is off the pillowcase – it's the only way out."

They listened carefully, but they couldn't hear anything.

"Let's try," said Kirsty. "If we're going to escape before he takes us to Jack Frost, we have to find the wand fast."

"Hold out your hands," said Daisy, "Let's find each other first."

Stretching out her hands in both directions, Rachel found Kirsty on her left and Daisy on her right.

"Let's crawl forwards with our
arms stretched out like this," she said.
"Hopefully one of us will find the wand
on our way."

They started to move slowly forwards.

The folds of cloth made good hiding
places, and it was hard to feel sure that
they had searched every crease.

"Nothing," sighed Kirsty when they
reached the bottom of the pillowcase.

"Let's try another way," said Rachel.

"I'll start in one corner and you two start in the other."

They crawled through the pillowcase again, and again they found no wand. Then they heard the distant crash of pots and pans.

"That's it!" squawked a loud voice. "I've sold the last bacon-and-egg roll. Time to go."

"We've run out of time!" cried Daisy. "What are we going to do now?"

Fast Magic

Suddenly, Kirsty saw something glimmering in the shadowy corner beside her. She lifted the cloth and saw a tiny puff of fairy dust coming from Daisy's wand.

"It's here!" she cried. "I've got it!"

Daisy crawled towards her and took the wand with a beaming smile.

105

"Clever wand!" she said. "Right, let's get out of here."

She pointed her wand at the pillowcase and said,

"Three fairies in a nasty scrape
Now need to make a fast escape.
Please help us leave this pillowcase
And give ourselves some breathing space!"

Instantly, a hole appeared in the white pillowcase. It grew bigger and bigger, until it was large enough for them to fit through.

Quickly, the fairies darted out of their
strange prison, and then Daisy closed the
hole with her wand. They could see the
shapes of the three goblins at the tent
entrance.

"Right, let's get these fairies back to
the Ice Castle," said one with a cackling
laugh. "Jack Frost had better reward us
for capturing three in one go!"

"There's the sleeping bag!" hissed
Kirsty, pointing to the furthest corner of
the tent. "Quick, let's grab it!"

They zoomed towards the purple
sleeping bag as the goblins began to
undo the tent zip.

"Come on, slowcoach," squawked
another goblin voice.

Daisy reached the sleeping bag as the
goblins elbowed their way into the tent.

As soon as she touched the bag, it shrank to fairy size and she tucked it under her arm.

"Too late!" cried Rachel in a triumphant voice.

The goblins let out howls of frustration.

"Give that back!" they yelled. "Thieves! Robbers!"

"Nonsense, said Daisy firmly. "This is my sleeping bag, and you are the ones who stole it."

"I caught you once," bawled the guard goblin. "I can do it again."

"I don't think so," said Daisy, shaking her head.

She waved her wand and Rachel and Kirsty returned to human size so quickly that it made them gasp. Suddenly their heads were pressed against the top of the tent.

"Let's get out of here," said Rachel. "It's starting to feel a bit cramped!"

She moved towards the goblins and they shuffled backwards.

"I'm getting really bored of this festival," the first goblin grumbled.

"I agree," said the second, glaring at the girls. "Too many humans!"

"Let's make a move before Jack Frost finds out about this pesky fairy getting the sleeping bag back," said the third. "He's going to spit thunderbolts!"

The goblins scrambled out of the
tent and raced off. Rachel and Kirsty
followed them out and Daisy fluttered
close behind.

"Look what a mess they've made," said
Kirsty with a groan.

The table where they had been serving
food was covered in dirty pots and pans,
and there was rubbish all over the grass.

"Are any humans watching?" asked Daisy.

The girls shook their heads, and Daisy gave her wand a little flick. Instantly the rubbish flew into the nearest bin, and the pots and pans were sparkling clean and stacked in neat piles.

Rachel and Kirsty grinned at each other.

"We did it," said Rachel. "That's two of your magical objects back where they belong, Daisy."

"I couldn't have done it without you," said Daisy. "Now I need to hurry back to Fairyland. When the sweet-dreams sleeping bag is back where it belongs, I will be able to do some more magic to fight against Jack Frost's bad-weather spell."

She waved her hand and then vanished in a tiny burst of candyfloss-coloured fairy dust. Almost at once, a few shafts of sunlight pierced through the dark cloud above.

"She's done it," said Kirsty, jumping up and down. "Her magic is stopping Jack Frost's spell from working!"

"But the black cloud is still there," Rachel replied, looking up. "I hope we can find the final magical object in time for tomorrow's concert. Without it, Jack Frost could still spoil things for everyone."

"We'll do it," said Kirsty, squeezing her best friend's hand. "I know we will!"

The
VIP Wristband

Contents

A Musical Breakfast

"I can hardly believe that it's the last day of the Rainbow Days Festival already," said Rachel, as she and Kirsty got dressed on Sunday morning. "It's gone so fast!"

"What have you enjoyed most so far?" Kirsty asked.

"Apart from our fairy adventures, you mean?" asked Rachel with a smile. "All the music has been brilliant. But today's final concert will be the best! The Angels and Groove Gang are performing, and Jacob Bright and Dakota May are doing a duet."

There were four different stages around the festival site and there was always someone performing on one of them. The biggest stage was at the centre of the festival, and that was where today's amazing concert would be held.

"I heard that The Angels are going to sing an old 80s song to fit in with today's theme," said Kirsty, twirling around in her neon ra-ra skirt. "I love these retro clothes!"

Rachel pulled on some legwarmers and

clapped her hands together.

"We're ready!" she said. "Let's make breakfast."

Mr and Mrs Walker were still asleep in their tent, so the girls quietly got out the camping stove and food. Soon they were eating a marvellous breakfast of toast, eggs, sausages, bacon and beans.

"This is delicious," said Rachel. "Now that Daisy has her sweet-dreams sleeping bag back, camp food tastes delicious again. I bet Mum and Dad are finding their

tent super-comfortable too. No wonder they're having a lie-in!"

Kirsty was looking at the dew on the grass sparkling in the sunshine.

"It looks as if it is going to be a perfect day," she said. "I hope that means Daisy's magic is stronger than Jack Frost's bad-weather spell."

The girls sat in silence, listening to birds singing in the trees around the campsite. There was no one else around.

"I love early mornings," said Rachel. "They're so …"

She paused as a high, clear voice joined in with the birds, singing the notes of their song. Looking up, the girls saw Daisy sitting in one of the silver birch trees, singing along with the blackbirds.

"… magical," finished Kirsty with a smile. "Hello, Daisy!"

The little fairy waved to her, but carried on singing for a few minutes more. The song was one of the most beautiful things that the girls had ever heard. At last Daisy finished the song on a happy, trilling note and fluttered down beside the girls.

"That was amazing," said Kirsty, as Daisy perched on an upturned bowl. "What were you singing?"

"It's a special part of the magic

I'm using to stop Jack Frost's bad
weather," Daisy explained. "It will keep
this morning how it is supposed to be –
sunny and bright – but it won't last all
day unless I get my VIP wristband back."

"Then we have to find it this morning,"
said Rachel. "We don't want this
afternoon's concert to be cancelled
because it's stormy!"

"If we don't find the VIP wristband, the
concert will be a disaster anyway," said
Daisy. "Until I get it back, none of the
bands will perform well. They might not
even turn up!"

Rachel and Kirsty exchanged alarmed
glances.

"Let's go to the main stage as soon as
we've finished breakfast," said Kirsty. "We
can ask if there are any problems with

the singers."

Rachel ate the last of her breakfast and stood up.

"We need to do the dishes before we go," she said. "Come on."

There was a stream at the bottom of the field where they had been doing their washing up. Daisy swooped under the brim of Rachel's sunhat to hide, and then the girls hurried to the stream. They had to start looking for the VIP wristband quickly – time was running out to save the concert!

The Clouds Gather

As soon as Rachel and Kirsty had done the washing up, they wrote a note to tell Rachel's parents where they had gone. Then they sped off towards the centre of the festival. When they got closer, they heard a loud whining sound.

"That's the sound system being tested," said Kirsty. "The concert organisers must be at the stage already."

When they reached the large stage, they saw six people sitting in a circle with their chins resting in their hands. The girls hurried up the stairs at the side of the stage and took a few steps towards the circle of people. A brown-haired woman in a long, flowery dress stood up.

"Can I help you?" she asked.

"We were just wondering how everything was going," said Rachel. "We're really excited about the concert later."

The woman gave them a weak smile, but they could see worry in her eyes.

"That's great," she said. "Everything's fine."

A bearded man stood up and put his hand on her shoulder.

"It's no use pretending, Sophie," he

132

said. "You might as well tell them the truth. People will find out soon enough anyway."

Sophie sighed.

"Josh is right – we don't know if there's going to *be* a concert," she said. "Three of today's acts haven't turned up, and that's not all."

"Two of the acts who *are* here have suddenly come down with sore throats and can't sing," added Josh.

"And out of the others, two have lost

their instruments and one has forgotten his songs," said Sophie. "Not to mention the fact that the sound system isn't working. It's a total disaster!"

"The first act is due on the stage in a couple of hours and we don't have a single performer," said Josh. "Even the weather's against us."

He pointed to a grey cloud that was about to block the sun and his shoulders slumped.

"Don't give up," said Kirsty. "There's still time for

everything to be OK."

But Sophie and Josh just exchanged disbelieving glances. Rachel squeezed her best friend's hand.

"The only way we can cheer them up is to find the VIP wristband and stop Jack Frost," she whispered. "Come on."

The girls ran down the stage steps and headed into the main festival site. It was busier now as the stalls were open and the festival crowds were appearing. Even though they were worried about finding the VIP

wristband, the girls couldn't help but gaze at all the amazing 80s outfits.

"I've never seen so many shoulder pads and neon colours in one place!" said Kirsty with a giggle.

"How are we going to spot green goblins among all these crowds and

colourful costumes?" Rachel asked.

"Keep trying," whispered Daisy
from beneath Rachel's sunhat.
"That grey cloud shows that my
magic is weakening without the
VIP wristband."

As she spoke, a chilly breeze started to

blow. All around them, people pulled their summer clothes more tightly around them.

"Brrr, I've got goose bumps," said Kirsty with a shiver.

"It's getting darker," said Rachel, scanning the crowds. "I still can't see any goblins, but they must be around here somewhere. Jack Frost ordered them to cause as much mischief at the festival as they could."

"The magical ice storm is getting

closer," Daisy exclaimed. "We have to keep looking!"

The Boastful Busker

Suddenly Kirsty let out a surprised squeak.

"Something hit me!" she cried. "Ouch!"

"Me too," said Rachel, looking up. "That stung!"

"It's hail," said Daisy with a groan. "The ice storm must be very close now."

The hail began to fall more steadily,

and people ran to take cover under
the workshop tents and stall canopies.
Everyone was shouting about the strange
weather.

"Over there!" cried Kirsty, pointing to
the nearest tent.

It had red-and-yellow stripes, and there
was a painted
wooden sign
outside it
saying
'Lost
Children
Wait
Here'.
The girls

squeezed into the crowd under the
canvas and waited for the hail to pass.
They could hear a busker playing the

guitar and singing somewhere nearby.

"Wow, he's amazing," said a girl next to Kirsty.

"Incredible!" said someone else in the crowd.

The girls stood up on their tiptoes and saw a short singer with his back to the entrance of the tent. He was wearing a shiny silver jumpsuit with enormous shoulder pads, and a wig of crimped blond hair. He looked very peculiar, but his

143

playing and singing were brilliant.

"He must have the VIP wristband," said Daisy. "There's no other way he could sound so perfect while it's missing."

"That means he must be a goblin," added Kirsty. "It's hard to tell underneath that enormous wig!"

Rachel jumped up to get a better view. She could see a long, green nose poking out from under the shaggy wig.

"He's definitely a goblin, and he's wearing something red on his wrist," she said, jumping up again. "Yes, it's a red wristband. We've found it!"

"That was easier than I thought," Kirsty said.

"Me too," said Daisy. "But the hard part is going to be getting it back!"

The hail had stopped, although the weather was getting colder and gloomier. As the crowd thinned out, Rachel pulled Kirsty out of the goblin's sight and the two of them sat down on the grass beside an unattended loom-band stall.

"We have to think of a way to get that wristband away from the goblin without him realising," said Rachel. "We need a brainwave!"

145

Daisy rubbed her head and Rachel frowned in thought, but it was no use. Kirsty gazed around the craft stalls, wondering what they should do. Opposite the loom-band stall was a large sign that said 'Relax with a facial!' At the stall, a young woman with pigtails was smearing a girl's face with a cucumber face mask.

"I think I've got an idea," said Kirsty in

a low voice. "Maybe if we could relax the goblin and make him close his eyes, he wouldn't notice us taking the wristband off."

"Kirsty, that's a brilliant idea!" said Rachel. "Daisy, will you disguise us as face-mask experts?"

"In a wink," said Daisy. "Duck down behind the loom-band stall for a moment."

The girls did as she asked, and when they popped their heads up a moment later, they looked very different.

They were wearing long flowery
dresses and each of them was wearing
a printed badge saying 'Facial Expert'.
Both of their shoulder bags were full of
face mask pots. The girls smiled at
each other.

"Let's go!" said Kirsty.

The goblin had stopped playing for a moment and was counting the money that he had collected in his hat.

"Excuse me," said Rachel, tapping him on the shoulder. "Would you like a relaxing face mask?"

"No," snapped the goblin, shaking her hand away. "Go and annoy someone else."

"But this would be free," said Kirsty, stepping forward. "Your music is so amazing that we would be honoured to be allowed to give you a facial."

The goblin puffed out his chest, and the silver jumpsuit glimmered.

"I *am* extremely good," he said.

"And you must be tired after such a fantastic performance," Rachel added. "A

facial will help you to relax, and you'll look and sing even better."

"I'm not sure that's possible," said the goblin, preening himself. "But you can try!"

The Ice Storm Arrives

Kirsty borrowed a chair from the Lost Kids Tent and the goblin sat down.

"I'll start with a strawberry face mask," said Kirsty, smearing pink goo all over his green face.

"I'll cover your eyes," said Rachel, pulling up two slices of cucumber from her bag.

The goblin leaned back in the chair.

"Ooh, that's cold!" he yelped as Rachel laid the cucumber on his eyes.

"Now, Daisy!" Kirsty whispered.

The Festival Fairy fluttered out from Kirsty's shoulder bag and hovered beside the goblin's arm. He was quite still, so she put her hands on the wristband and began to move it.

Slowly, slowly, a millimetre at a time, Daisy eased the wristband downwards. Rachel and Kirsty

chattered to the goblin about facials
as well as they could, and all the time
the wristband came closer and closer to
being theirs.

"Almost," Daisy murmured. "Almost!"

"WHAT'S GOING ON HERE?"

A furious yell made them all jump, and
the goblin shot out of
his seat, trembling.
Jack Frost was
standing
behind them,
purple in
the face
with anger,
holding
Daisy in
his hand.
Everyone had

been so busy looking at the wristband, they hadn't noticed him arrive.

"Are you blind?" he bellowed, stomping towards the goblin with each word. "Are you stupid? You nearly lost the wristband to this pesky little fairy. You idiot! You numbskull! Give it to me!"

Jack Frost snatched the wristband and put it on. The goblin scurried away before he got into any more trouble.

"Let her go!" cried Rachel, jumping up to try to

reach the little fairy.

"The VIP wristband is mine and so is
she!" Jack Frost cackled. "It's time you
learned that you can't get the better of
the stupendous Jack Frost!"

As he laughed, the sky turned black.
Hailstones began to beat down again,
but this time even more heavily.
People started to run for cover, and the
stallholders abandoned their stalls.

"The music concert will be cancelled!" said Kirsty with a groan.

"I've won!" Jack Frost crowed, leaping around as if he were doing a jig. "I've won!"

He held Daisy hidden in his hand as the girls jumped up around him, trying to force him to release her.

"You can't keep her prisoner like this!" Kirsty cried.

"Give back the VIP wristband!" said

Rachel. "It doesn't belong to you!"

"The festival is OVER!" Jack Frost yelled at them. "The fairy and the wristband are mine now, and you silly humans have LOST!"

"Give them back!" the girls exclaimed, trying to ignore the stinging hail.

Suddenly they heard a deep voice behind them.

"What's going on here?"

Jack Frost's Comeuppance

A burly security guard grabbed Jack Frost by the scruff of his scrawny neck and marched him under a nearby tent awning. The girls followed, relieved to escape the hail.

"Let me go, you idiot!" bawled the Ice Lord.

The man frowned.

"That's not very polite," he said. "I'm one of the festival security guards, and it's my job to stop troublemakers like you. You should be ashamed of yourself, stealing a wristband from children. Give it back right now!"

"Mind your own business!" Jack Frost shouted.

"This *is* my business," said the security guard. "The festival organisers use wristbands to check that people have paid to get in, and it's my job to make sure that everyone is wearing one."

He hadn't noticed that both the girls were already wearing their festival wristbands! They hurriedly hid their wrists behind their backs.

"Get off me!" hollered Jack Frost. "I'll

freeze you to the spot! I'll stop you in
your tracks!"

He pulled his wand from under his
cloak and pointed it over his shoulder
at the security guard. Rachel and Kirsty
gasped, but the security guard just
yanked the wand from
Jack Frost's hand.

"You rock
stars are all
crazy," he
said, looking
at the wand.
"You think
you can get
away with
anything, but
not here!
I don't know

what this silly little toy is, but you're not getting it back until you return the wristband to these girls."

Without his wand, there was no way that Jack Frost could get free from the strong security guard. He wriggled and squirmed, but he couldn't escape.

"OK," he said, with a big fake smile. "Let me go first and then I'll give back the wristband."

"No chance," said the security guard. "You give it back first."

"FINE" Jack Frost snapped.

He had to release Daisy to be able to pull the wristband off.

She zoomed behind
Rachel before
the security
guard could see
her, and Jack
Frost flung the
wristband at
Kirsty's feet.

"Thank you!"
Rachel said
to the security
guard.

"No problem," he replied.

Jack Frost shook his fist in the security guard's face, showing his bare, bony arm.

"Let me go!" he demanded.

But the security guard was staring at his wrist.

"Hey, you're not wearing a festival

wristband!" he exclaimed. "So *that's* why you were trying to steal one from these girls. Well, no wristband, no festival! You can have your toy back when you're off the festival grounds."

He marched Jack Frost away, and the girls joined hands and spun around. The Ice Lord's indignant howls faded into the distance.

"Thank goodness for security guards!" said Rachel with a laugh.

Daisy fluttered around them, laughing

and smiling. Kirsty
handed her the
VIP wristband
and it shrunk
to fairy size,
just as the
sun began
to come
out. The hail
on the ground
melted away in the
sunshine.

"Everything's back to normal," said
Rachel in a delighted voice.

"Not quite," said Daisy with a smile.

She waved her wand and the girls'
disguises disappeared. They were wearing
their 80s outfits again.

"Now you're ready for the concert," she

said. "And I have to return to Fairyland
and get ready for the Grand Fairy
Festival. It can go ahead now, thanks to
you. You've been wonderful!"

"I hope you have an amazing time,"
said Rachel.

"Goodbye, Daisy," said Kirsty.

The little fairy smiled at them, and
then she had vanished in the blink of an
eye. At that moment, the girls heard the
twang of an electric guitar echoing from
large speakers. It came from the direction
of the large central stage.

"The sound system must be working!"
cried Rachel.

"And the musicians are practising,"
Kirsty added.

A line of tour buses was bumping over
the field towards them – the missing

bands had arrived.

"It looks as if everything's going to be OK," said Rachel, squeezing Kirsty's hand.

A short time later the girls were dancing in front of the stage with Mr and Mrs Walker while The Angels opened the concert. The crowd cheered and sang along, and the sun shone in a cloudless sky.

"This is the happiest festival I could ever imagine," exclaimed Kirsty, putting her arm through Rachel's. "I can't wait for next year!"

Now it's time for Kirsty and
Rachel to help...

Catherine
the Fashion Princess Fairy

Read on for a sneak peek...

"Three cheers for the princesses!" shouted
an excited tourist.

Outside the royal gates, Rachel Walker
and Kirsty Tate cheered along with the
rest of the crowd, and then gazed up
at the palace in the heart of the city.
The elegant, spiral bars were painted
gold, and decorated with tiny silver
hummingbirds.

"Isn't it amazing to think that your
mum's friend is in there right now, talking
to the youngest princess?" said Rachel to

her best friend.

Kirsty nodded. Everyone loved the three princesses, but the youngest – Princess Edie – was their favourite.

"I wonder which room is hers," she said.

"I think it's that one," said Rachel, pointing up at an open window where white curtains were billowing in the summer breeze.

"Bee has such a different life from us," said Kirsty. "I can't imagine what it must be like to be a fashion stylist and help a princess decide what to wear every day!"

"Her house is amazing too," Rachel added. "I wonder what it's like to live in the city."

"We're going to find out this weekend," said Kirsty with a grin.

Rachel and Kirsty were visiting the city for the weekend with Kirsty's parents.

They were staying with Bee, who was an old friend of Kirsty's mother from university.

"Bee always has such interesting stories to tell about the princesses," Kirsty went on. "It's so much fun hearing about what their lives are like. She loves Princess Edie best of all."

"I wish she'd hurry up," said Rachel, gazing up at the window with the billowing curtains. "I can't wait to start sightseeing. I want to visit all the most famous places in the city."

The girls were waiting with Kirsty's parents to meet Bee when she had finished in the palace. Mr and Mrs Tate were taking photos of the sentry guard, and Kirsty slipped her arm through Rachel's.

"It's very different from the palace

in Fairyland, isn't it?" she said in a soft voice.

Rachel smiled, thinking of the beautiful pink palace where Queen Titania and King Oberon lived. They had been friends of Fairyland ever since they first met on Rainspell Island, and they loved sharing their magical secret.

"It's exciting being here," said Rachel. "But I hope that we get to see the Fairyland Palace again soon."

"You may see it sooner than you think," said a silvery voice.

The girls jumped in surprise, and then stepped closer to the gate. An exquisitely dressed fairy was standing with her arm around one of the spiral bars.

The little fairy was wearing a flowing dress of green chiffon, with a sparkling belt clasp and delicate lacy sleeves. A tiny pillbox hat was perched at an angle on her head, and her glossy brown hair coiled over her shoulder.

"Hello," she said. "I'm Catherine the Fashion Princess Fairy."

Read **Catherine the Fashion Princess Fairy** to find out what adventures are in store for Kirsty and Rachel!

Join in the magic online by signing up
to the Rainbow Magic fan club!

Meet the fairies, play games and
get sneak peeks at the latest books!

There's fairy fun for everyone at

www.rainbowmagicbooks.co.uk

You'll find great activities, competitions, stories and
fairy profiles, and also a special newsletter.

Find a fairy with
your name!